D0597485

Big Like Me

Anna Grossnickle Hines

Big Like Me

Greenwillow Books  New York

Watercolor paints and colored pencils were used for the full-color art.
The text type is Pacella.

Library of Congress Cataloging-in-Publication Data
Hines, Anna Grossnickle.
Big like me / by Anna Grossnickle Hines.
p.   cm.
Summary: A boy tells his baby sister all the
things he will show her as she grows, from snow and
bouncing high to making faces and blowing out candles.
ISBN 0-688-08354-4.   ISBN 0-688-08355-2 (lib. bdg.)
[1. Babies—Fiction.   2. Brothers and sisters—Fiction.]
I. Title.   PZ7.H572Bi 1989
[E]—dc19   88-18772   CIP   AC

TO KATLYN RUTH AND
JULIE CHRISTINE,
THE NEW BABIES

Hello Baby,
little tiny baby.
This is me.
I'm going to show you everything.

I'll show you snow
and listening to stories.

And bouncing high.

I'll show you baby rattles
and squeaky toys
and my best teddy bear.
Hi there, old bear.

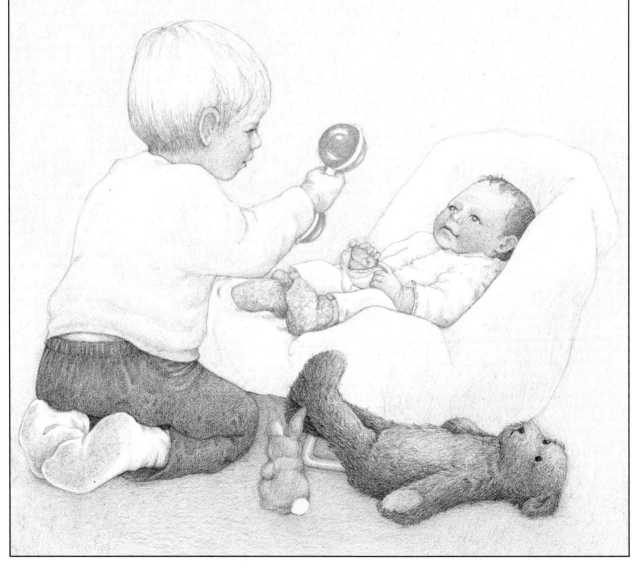

I'll show you laps
and taking naps.

I'll show you springtime trees
with new green leaves
and caterpillars crawling.

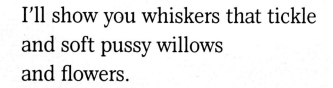

I'll show you whiskers that tickle
and soft pussy willows
and flowers.

I'll show you rolling balls
and building blocks
and peek-a-boo.
I see you!

I'll show you nose to nose
and toes to toes
and rolling over.

I'll show you pat-a-cake
and upside down
and laughing loud.

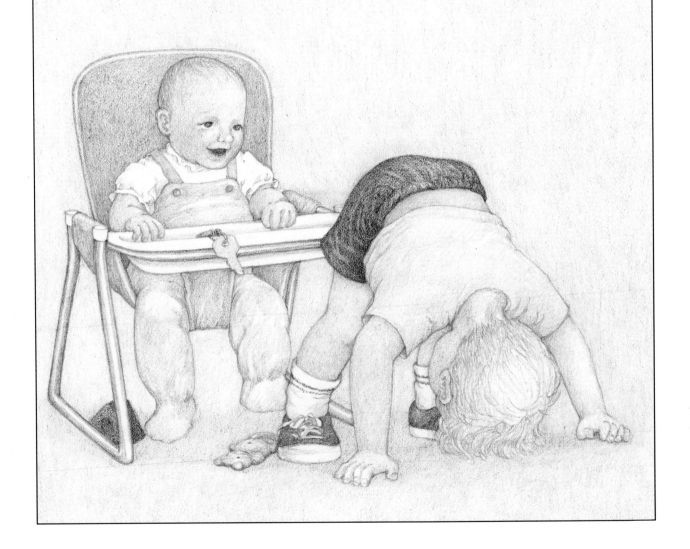

I'll show you grass in your toes,
a cold wet nose,
and a doggie kiss.

I'll show you splashing
and pouring
and filling the cup
to pour some more.

I'll show you hide and seek.
You mustn't peek.

I'll show you going for walks,
jumping off rocks,
and the big, long slide.

Wheee!
Look out for me!

I'll show you crawling
under chairs

and climbing up.

I'll show you riding high.
We'll touch the sky.

And falling leaves
and beetles
and rain.

I'll show you eating crackers
and drinking from a cup.
Just tip it up.

I'll show you blowing bubbles
and saying hi and bye-bye-bye.

I'll show you squishing dough
and patting it flat
and cutting cookies
and tasting.

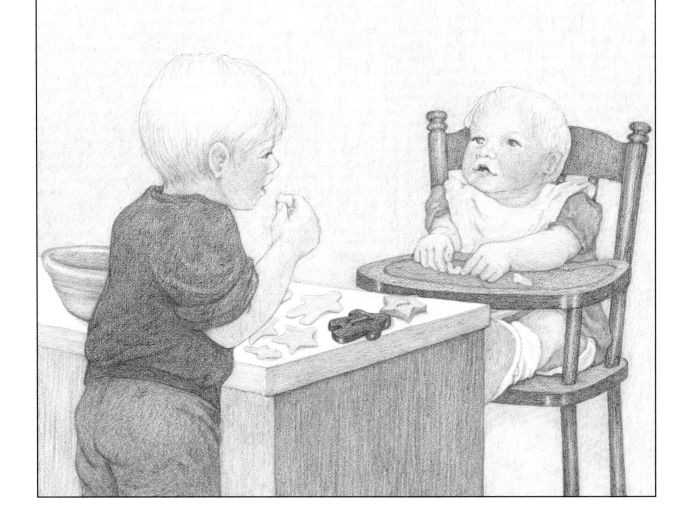

I'll show you shiny balls
and jingle bells
and singing songs.

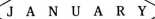

I'll show you making faces
and having races here to there.
I'll let you win.

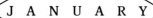

I'll show you blowing out candles
and opening packages.
Happy birthday, Baby.
I'll show you growing big
like me!

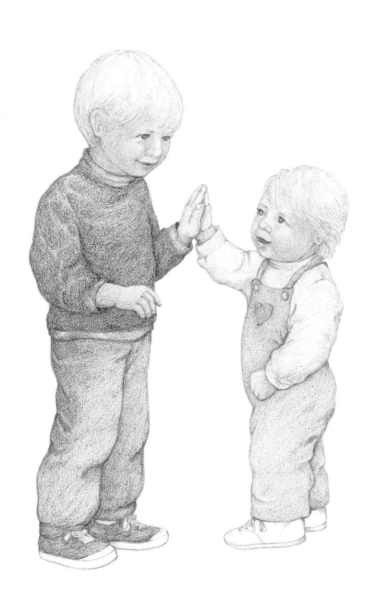